S0-AIB-195

QUICKREADS

THE PLOT

JANICE GREENE

SADDLEBACK
EDUCATIONAL PUBLISHING

◼QUICKREADS

SADDLEBACK
EDUCATIONAL PUBLISHING
www.sdlback.com

ISBN-13: 978-1-61651-204-0
ISBN-10: 1-61651-204-0
eBook: 978-1-60291-926-6

Printed in Guangzhou, China
0511/05-27-11

15 14 13 12 11   2 3 4 5 6

■ ■ ■

Tara Tiongson looked at her calendar and gasped. The deadline was in just two days, and she hadn't even received her application yet! She ran downstairs and found her mom and sister watching TV.

"Mom!" she cried. "Didn't I get anything in the mail from the Summer Bridge Program?"

"What?" said her mother, reaching for her coffee mug without taking her eyes from the TV screen.

"The Summer Bridge Program," said Tara. "Didn't it come in the mail?"

"Hon, I can't be expected to know about every little thing that comes in the mail. I don't know why we get so much junk—" her mother grumbled.

"Mom! You threw it out, didn't you?" said Tara.

Tara's older sister, Kimmie, glared at her and reached for the remote to turn up the volume.

"Oh, honey, I don't know," said her mother. "Why's it so important?"

Tara gritted her teeth at her mother's favorite expression. "Mom," she went on, "I want to apply for a special math program. I'd get to take classes at the university. It's important to *me!*" But her mom had her eyes glued to the TV. Corny music was swelling as a tall blond man entered the room.

"It's Brad!" Kimmie said. "Remember, Mom? He's supposed to be dead."

Mom said, "Oh, yeah. Brad—"

Tara gave up and went into the kitchen. As always, it was a mess. But this morning she just didn't have the energy to clean up. She looked for cereal, finally finding a box on the stove. But all the bowls were dirty, crusted with bits of dried food. So Tara filled a mug with cereal and grabbed milk from the refrigerator. As she opened the carton, she noticed a sour smell. Disgusted, she dropped the carton in the sink, where the bad milk slowly chugged out over a pile of dirty plates, candy wrappers, and lumps of clotted rice.

Kimmie wandered in and began to search for cereal, too.

"Here's some," Tara said, handing her the cereal box. "Kimmie, could you clean up the kitchen for once?"

"Not now. I'm wiped out. *You* try an eight-hour job sometime," Kimmie said.

"That's not fair, Kimmie! I've got work *plus* tons of homework every night!" Tara shot back.

"Homework's a waste! When you graduate, you're just going to get a regular old job, anyway," Kimmie said.

"I don't want a *job,*" Tara insisted. "I want a career."

"Oh, *please!*" Kimmie said mockingly. "You keep trying to act like you're better than Mom and me! But you're not! I can tell you, baby—you're just the same!"

Tara opened her mouth for a smart retort, but then decided against it.

Fighting with her sister would only make her bad mood worse. She stomped out of the room, grabbed her books, and ran out to catch the bus to school. Her stomach was growling.

■ ■ ■

Just before math class, Derek Rodis caught up with Tara in the hall. "Did you send in your application yet?" he asked excitedly.

"No," said Tara. "I never got it."

Derek looked alarmed. "You *didn't?* You should call them!"

"That's a good idea," said Tara, hoping her mother had paid the phone bill. Last month they'd been without phone service for two weeks.

As she went to her seat, Tara's friends surrounded her. "Why are you talking to that geeky guy Derek?" Pati teased. "He's so *homely!*"

"The word is *ugly*," Kaitlin chimed in. "I agree. Why waste your breath on ugly guys?" she added.

Tara looked over at Derek, who was bent over his math book. He was a thin guy with big ears and an intense look. He *wasn't* ugly! Once he'd told her he'd gotten in trouble for getting a B on his report card. She wondered what it was like, having parents who expected nothing less than straight A's.

As Mr. Ferris started lecturing, Tara felt boredom settle over her like a heavy blanket. Last year, when she'd been a sophomore, Mr. Marinucci taught math. Every class had been exciting. One day, after they'd done a unit in architecture, Mr. Marinucci had caught up with her in the hall. "Tara," he said, "you seem to have a real talent for architecture. You're quite gifted in math, and your drawings are— wonderful, exceptional! Have you ever given any thought to architecture as a career?"

The truth was that Tara hadn't considered *any* career. She only knew she didn't want to end up like her mother and sister.

Mr. Marinucci's suggestions opened up a whole new world to her. She began to dream of the steel and glass buildings downtown. She imagined a gleaming white office building that was hers alone.

That was last year. Although the dream was still there, every day, during Mr. Ferris' lectures, it faded a little. Still, she was hopeful enough to go up to his desk after class.

"Mr. Ferris, I wanted to apply for the Summer Bridge Program—" She stopped at his blank look.

"Summer Bridge Program?" he asked. "What's that? Does it have something to do with math?"

"Never mind," Tara said.

She left the classroom and hurried down the jammed hallway. Suddenly, she felt like she couldn't get out of Maxwell Senior High soon enough.

Kimmie had dropped out in her junior year. Maybe she'd felt the way Tara did now—that she simply couldn't take another minute of slamming lockers and yelling kids, peeling paint, and the heavy, stale odors of lunch leftovers.

■ ■ ■

As Tara walked into the back room at Lupo's 1-Hour Photo and Copy, Josie greeted her with bad news. "Billy called in sick, Tara. Mrs. Lee said she wants you to close up tonight."

"And *you* can't?" Tara asked.

"She said *you,*" Josie said smugly.

Tara put her backpack on the floor. There was very little space in the back room. Most of it was taken up by the film processor, the big machine that developed film. There were also heavy rolls of photographic paper and bottles of chemicals stacked all around.

The front room, where customers came in, was crowded, too. The printer processor, a big machine that printed the photos on paper, took up most of the space. But there was also a bulky copy machine—and behind the counter, a cash register. Next to the window was a tall plastic plant that Mrs. Leealways decorated at Christmas.

Frowning, Tara looked through the orders to be filled that night. The film had been developed yesterday, but so far today only a few prints had been made.

"Josie—" Tara began.

Tara's co-worker turned and looked at her, her eyes wide and innocent. Tara was sure Josie had plenty of excuses for not doing her work. But right now she was too tired to hear them.

"Never mind," Tara said with a sigh.

Tara loaded the negatives in the machine and got it ready to go. Josie was busy with the copier, an order sheet in her hand. Tara got out her life science book. There was a test tomorrow and she had to study. She read two paragraphs, and then Josie was at her side.

"Look. I was saving these until you got here," Josie said. She shoved some photos at Tara. It looked like a scene from a slumber party. A bathroom was jammed with girls in pajamas, some holding beer bottles. One girl, perched on the edge of the toilet, was getting her ears pierced. Tara stared at the blurry close-up. The girl's face seemed to be half-laughing, half-scared.

Josie pulled the photo away and stuck another in Tara's face. "Look at this one—she's throwing up!" Josie howled with laughter.

"Josie, we shouldn't be gawking at people's pictures. They're private!" Tara said, frowning.

"Oh, come on! When they come out, we have to check them over anyway. What's the difference?" Josie asked.

"It just isn't *right!* When people send in their film, they don't want to think that strangers are making fun of their photographs," Tara said.

"At least I don't make copies—like Billy does. Remember those people in the hot tub?" Josie giggled.

Tara rolled her eyes and said, "Don't remind me!"

Then the door opened, and two women

came in to get their photos. Tara rang up the sale and quickly went back to her science book.

The women leaned on the counter, looking through their photos. "Oh, this is *adorable!*" one of the women cried. "You have to send this one to Mom."

"Look at this one of the baby in his little overalls," said the other woman.

Tara slammed her science book closed. She couldn't concentrate. She made a note to stop by the store on the way home and get some milk. Then she wondered if she had anything clean to wear tomorrow. She didn't. Suddenly it all seemed too hard. She felt so tired and discouraged, she wanted to cry.

Tara saw that Josie was humming as she watched the copier staple and spit out copies. How different her life was from Tara's! Josie actually ironed her clothes. She always had a pretty haircut, too. Since dropping out of school, Josie worked full time at Lupo's. She had time to fix herself up, to buy clothes, to read a magazine. She didn't have to go to the creepy laundromat late at night and do her homework there.

"It's just too much!" Tara thought angrily. School, work, home. *Home.* If she dropped out of school, she could fix up the house, make it look nice. She could help her mother find a job, a good job she could hang onto. Maybe she could even figure out how to help Mom remember things—to cope with life.

"I could get you a job doing data entry anytime," Kimmie kept telling her. Kimmie liked her supervisor, and she'd gotten a raise last year. With a weary sigh, Tara thought about it. If she quit school tomorrow, she could stay in bed and sleep instead of struggling through another day. Just now, the towering glass and steel offices downtown seemed as unreachable as another planet.

Tara heard the sounds of first photographs coming out of the printer. She grabbed an envelope and reached for the first one—and her eyes went wide with shock.

"Josie," she said slowly. "Look at this." She laid the photos out on the counter.

Josie looked over the snapshots and whistled. *"Whoa!"* she yelled out.

■ ■ ■

The young man in the photo was bare to the waist. He wore camouflage pants and military-style boots. He was surrounded by guns—and more.

"Those contraptions with wires," Tara said. "You think those are bombs?"

Josie snickered. "Yeah," she agreed. "This guy could be one sick puppy."

"Josie, this is *serious,*" Tara said in a shaky voice.

"Do you see that thing with the nails sticking out?" Tara went on. "That's a kind of bomb. When it explodes, the nails shoot out like bullets. And see that gun right there?" She pointed. "That's a sawed-off shotgun. I saw one just like it on TV. They're totally illegal. We gotta call the police!"

"Now, wait a minute," Josie said. "We don't *really* know what's going on."

"Get real! You think all this stuff's for deer

hunting?" Tara cried.

"Tara, for a smart girl you aren't very sophisticated. Suppose the guy is innocent. If we call the cops on him, we could get in trouble," Josie said.

"But what if he *isn't?* Suppose he's planning to *use* these weapons? He could kill a lot of people!" Tara said.

"Oh, come on, Tara! Look at this guy's face. Does he *look* like some kind of mass murderer?" said Josie.

Tara had to admit that he didn't. The young man had an ordinary face. He actually looked like the quiet type. His expressionless eyes stared levelly at the camera.

"Hey, I know what," Josie went on. "He's probably into that game, *Fortress.*"

Tara shrugged and shook her head. "What's Fortress?"

"It's a video game. The object is to collect all the weapons you can. My little brother plays it," said Josie.

"You really think it's a game?"

"Yeah," said Josie. "Look, you're always

saying we should respect our customers' privacy. So let's do it—or that guy could sue us, big time."

"I guess he could," Tara admitted.

"Right!" said Josie. "So why take a chance of getting in trouble? Why's it so important that *you* have to do it?"

Why's it so important? Those awful words again! Anger rose in Tara like a hot bubble as she heard her mother's favorite expression. "Because people could *die!*" Tara cried out.

"You don't have to yell!" Josie snapped. "Okay! Fine. Do whatever you want. Just leave me out of it."

"Don't worry," Tara said coldly.

Josie gave her a disgusted look and reached for her coat and purse. Her shift wasn't over for another 20 minutes, but Tara decided to let her go.

After Josie stormed out the door, Tara rummaged under the counter for the phone book. She no longer felt tired. First, she'd call the police. Then she'd go over her science until she knew it perfectly. First thing tomorrow, she'd call up the Summer Bridge Program and ask them if they'd fax her an application at school. If she had any questions, she'd call Derek Rodis. Maybe she'd ask him to meet her in the library before the next big test. Her friends were fun—but all they talked about were boys and clothes. She needed a friend like Derek, too.

A pink sweater was lying on the counter— Josie had forgotten it. Tara picked it up and headed for the back room. But then the door opened and a customer walked in. It was *him*.

For a long moment, Tara could do nothing but stare. Her heart pounded in her chest, but she forced a smile. The photographs were still laid out on the counter. As the young man looked for his claim ticket, Tara covered up the photos with Josie's sweater.

■ ■ ■

When the young man held out his ticket, Tara saw that his name was Ryan Sayos.

Tara stalled. Her mind was racing as she pretended to look through the plastic bin that held the envelopes. She had to do something to stop him, but *what?*

"I don't scc them here, Mr. Sayos," she said. "I'll check to see if they're in the back room." Behind the counter, she grabbed the phone and spun around quickly, hiding it with her body.

With trembling fingers, she closed the door to the back room—and quickly punched in 911.

"I need help," she muttered when the emergency operator came on. "There's a man here who's planning something dangerous. He's in the store—*now!*"

"Where are you located?" the 911 operator asked calmly.

Then the door to the back room flew open and the young man stepped in. He was holding a knife!

He jerked his head at her, signaling that she should hang up. Nodding her head, Tara tossed the phone to him and he turned it off.

"Don't try anything," he warned. His voice was very soft and as cold as ice.

"What are you going to do?" she said.

His face was deadly calm. "You're all going to die," he said.

"All of us?" Tara said. She had to keep him talking. She'd read that somewhere.

"Everyone," he said. "Every little rat in a cage who's pretending to be so important. It's so pathetic—all the stupid schemes and plans you make. They turn to dust! They mean nothing! Your lives are useless, *empty!"*

He stroked his cheek with the knife blade, as if he loved the cool feel of it. She watched him, feeling helpless.

"What should we do?" she asked.

"Just die! *Disappear!* Wipe your pathetic, ugly selves from the face of the earth! Clean the planet!" he said.

"What's your name again?" she asked. He glared at her, and she knew she'd said the wrong thing.

"Get my pictures, *now!"* he ordered.

"They're not there," she protested. "They haven't been printed yet."

"Look again," he barked as he walked behind her to the counter. Tara went through the plastic bin one more time, while he watched over her shoulder. She went through half the photos, then three-fourths. "Stupid, stupid," Sayos kept muttering softly over her shoulder. She could feel his breath on her neck. *Think,* she told herself. She had to keep thinking or he might—

Then a shadow appeared outside the door. Sayos crouched behind the counter. She felt the knife blade lightly poking her ankle. When the door opened, a man in his fifties walked in. He had a thin, pinched face and a nervous manner.

"Billings," he said shortly, thrusting his ticket at Tara.

Tara found his photographs, and he pulled out his wallet. She grabbed a scrap of paper and wrote, *"Help—I'm being held hostage."* She slid the paper across the counter to the impatient man.

The man's eyes darted over her suspiciously. He gave her his money and snatched the envelope of photos.

"Would you like a bag?" she asked. Her eyes pleaded with him—but he wouldn't look at her face!

He shook his head and left.

The door closed. "Someone else is coming," she whispered. She glanced down at the young man crouching behind the counter. Then, almost without thinking, she grabbed the phone and slammed it down on his head.

Sayos roared, and she sprang away, around the counter and toward the front of the shop. He grabbed at her waist, but she twisted away from him. She seized the plastic plant around its middle and swung its heavy base at Sayos, banging his knees. He staggered and swore. Then she rammed the base of the plant right into the door. The glass shattered. *"Help!"* she screamed. *"Police!"*

■ ■ ■

Sayos tackled her and knocked her to the floor. He held her down, the knife poised just over her chest. Tara grabbed his knife hand and pushed against him desperately, her arm shaking from the effort. Glancing at his eyes, she looked away quickly, frightened by the furious intensity she saw there.

"In one minute, you'll be a dead rat," he gasped. Now Tara saw that the flying glass from the door had cut his neck. A drop of blood fell on her chin.

"No!" she screamed. *"Help! Help!"*

They heard footsteps outside. Suddenly, Sayos sprang up and tossed his knife on the floor. Two women joggers walked in, followed by a man in a suit.

Sayos turned to them. "Help me! That girl pulled a knife on me!" he cried.

"That's a lie!" Tara yelled.

"Look!" said Sayos, pulling aside his collar to show his bloody neck.

One of the joggers, a stocky woman with

very short gray hair, frowned questioningly at Tara.

The man moved in front of the door, as if to block Tara's way. When she saw the suspicion in his face, a cold shock of fear went through her.

Then Tara suddenly remembered the photographs. "I can prove he's lying!" she cried out. Throwing aside Josie's sweater, she snatched up the photographs from the counter.

Sayos threw her a fiery look and dashed out the door.

They all went after him, but he ran like the wind.

At the end of the street, Tara saw two men working on a car.

"*Get him!*" Tara screamed. "Don't let him get away!"

The guys looked up and saw Sayos being chased by four people.

"*Get him!*" Tara yelled again.

They did. Sayos dodged and swerved, but one guy grabbed him by the arm.

Sayos swung out at him, but the man held on. One of the women joggers arrived and grabbed Sayos' wrist. By then, he was completely surrounded. The man in the suit pulled a cell phonc from his jacket and called the police.

Sayos stood passively, his head slumped forward.

■ ■ ■

The next few hours were a blur. When the police came, Tara told her story again and again. By the time they drove her home, it was 1:00 in the morning. She was embarrassed, as always, to have people see where she lived. The house needed paint, and the yard was nothing but weeds. In the driveway was the rusting car her uncle had given Mom last year. But Mom had forgotten to put oil in it—and after a month, the engine was ruined. Someone had stolen the tires.

Tara thanked the officers and hurried out of the police car.

Kimmie was asleep on the couch, and Mom was watching TV.

"Hi, honey," her mom said sleepily.

"You'll never believe what happened, Mom. This guy brought in these really sick photos—"

Her mom interrupted, "Honey, you didn't remember to go to the store, by any chance, did you?"

"Mom, it looked like this guy was actually getting ready to *kill* a lot of people," Tara went on.

"Did you see this?" her mom said, gesturing toward the TV.

Tara got up and snapped off the TV. "Mom, *listen!* I really want you to hear this," she insisted.

Kimmie sat up. "What time is it?" she asked in a groggy voice.

Tara ignored her. "When I was at work—" she began. Her mother and sister listened while she told the whole story. When she finished, Kimmie cried, "How could you do that, Tara? It's a miracle that loony didn't kill you!"

"Kimmie's right, hon," Mom said. "The police probably would have caught him at some point. You didn't have to go and risk your life."

"I thought you'd be proud of me," Tara said bitterly. "Silly me. I should have known better."

"Well, excuse me if we don't just bow down in front of you!" Kimmie snapped. She got up from the couch and walked off in a huff. "I'm going to bed," she said over her shoulder.

Mom gave Tara a watery smile. "Honey, don't be upset. It's just that when I think of you lying on the floor and that man with the knife—" She shuddered. "If you'd just let him have his pictures in the first place—"

Tara opened her mouth to say, "He might have escaped!" but she stayed silent. She got up, saying, "Well, I'm alive anyway. See you tomorrow."

Mom gave her a vague, sweet smile. "I sure am glad you're alive, hon," she said. Her eyes were wet.

Tara leaned forward and kissed her cheek. "I'm glad, too, Mom," she said.

■ ■ ■

In her room, Tara lay down, not even bothering to change her clothes. She slept like a rock until Kimmie bounced on her bed the next morning.

"Tara! They talked about you on TV!" Kimmie yelled.

Tara sat up with a jerk and looked at the clock. "Oh, no!" she said. "I'm late!"

"There's no school, Tara. It's closed! That guy Sayos was gonna plant bombs in the gym. The police found a floorplan in his room," Kimmie went on.

"School's closed?" Tara said.

"They want to make sure he hadn't placed any bombs already," Kimmie explained. "I bet the news people are gonna come here. Maybe they'll bring a TV camera! And just look at me! I'm gonna put on my good blue dress."

Jumping up from the bed, Kimmie stopped and faced her sister. "I'm sorry about what

I said yesterday," she said softly. "I didn't mean that."

"It's okay," Tara said. "I should help more. I know Mom needs—"

Kimmie interrupted. "Don't worry about Mom! You just worry about school. You need to keep at it—'cause you're smart. Don't end up at a dead-end job like Mom and me," she said.

"Oh, Kimmie," Tara cried. She reached across the bed and pulled her sister into her arms. "You're not Mom. I mean, I love her—"

"I love her, too. Don't worry about us. We'll survive," Kimmie said.

Then the phone rang, and they heard their mother answer. A few seconds later, she burst into the room, startling them. Their mother never burst in anywhere.

"Tara!" she said breathlessly. "It's someone from the mayor's office. They want you to come downtown." Tara saw something on Mom's face she couldn't ever remember seeing before: *respect*.

Tara got up and took the phone from

her mother. "Downtown, here I come," she whispered. Today she was being invited downtown as a celebrity. But tomorrow, she promised herself, she would *belong* there.

■ ■ ■

EDITOR'S NOTE

This story was inspired by a real person who foiled a plan to massacre dozens of people at De Anza Community College in Cupertino, California.

Kelly Bennett is an 18-year-old student at San Jose State University who was working part-time as a photo processor at a drugstore in San Jose. On January 29, 2001, Kelly noticed photographs of Al DeGuzman, dressed in black, posing with a sawed-off shotgun and dozens of bombs.

"This was the scariest thing I'd ever seen," Kelly said. "I was 100 percent positive that this guy could be truly dangerous, so I decided to call the police."

Bennett's boss at the store was hesitant

about making a call to the police. "He was kind of iffy—he didn't want to make a decision right away," said Kelly. "So I asked my dad." Kelly called her father, Bob Bennett, a 17-year police veteran, for advice. He told her to call the police, so Kelly called 911. "I knew it was the right thing to do," she said.

Kelly made the call at 6:00 P.M. It was a few hours later when DeGuzman, a 19-year-old student at De Anza, came to pick up his photographs. Kelly was able to stall him until the police arrived at the store. Just as in the story, DeGuzman noticed the officers and tried to escape—but he was captured.

Between 3:30 and 4:00 A.M. on January 30, police searched DeGuzman's house. They seized 30 pipe bombs, 20 Molotov cocktails, numerous firearms, and a large amount of ammunition. They also found a map of De Anza College and a cassette tape. On the tape, DeGuzman described his plot to plant bombs around the campus the morning of January 30.